Dear Parent:

Congratulations! Your child is taking the first steps on an exciting journey. The destination? Independent reading!

STEP INTO READING® will help your child get there. The program offers five steps to reading success. Each step includes fun stories and colorful art. There are also Step into Reading Sticker Books, Step into Reading Math Readers, Step into Reading Write-In Readers, Step into Reading Phonics Readers, and Step into Reading Phonics First Steps! Boxed Sets—a complete literacy program with something for every child.

Learning to Read, Step by Step!

Ready to Read Preschool–Kindergarten
• big type and easy words • rhyme and rhythm • picture clues
For children who know the alphabet and are eager to begin reading.

Reading with Help Preschool–Grade 1
• basic vocabulary • short sentences • simple stories
For children who recognize familiar words and sound out new words with help.

Reading on Your Own Grades 1–3
• engaging characters • easy-to-follow plots • popular topics
For children who are ready to read on their own.

Reading Paragraphs Grades 2–3
• challenging vocabulary • short paragraphs • exciting stories
For newly independent readers who read simple sentences with confidence.

Ready for Chapters Grades 2–4
• chapters • longer paragraphs • full-color art
For children who want to take the plunge into chapter books but still like colorful pictures.

STEP INTO READING® is designed to give every child a successful reading experience. The grade levels are only guides. Children can progress through the steps at their own speed, developing confidence in their reading, no matter what their grade.

Remember, a lifetime love of reading starts with a single step!

For birds of a feather,
Ramona and Leo
—A.J.

Visit us on the Web!
www.stepintoreading.com
www.randomhouse.com/kids

Educators and librarians, for a variety of teaching tools, visit us at
www.randomhouse.com/teachers

Library of Congress Cataloging-in-Publication Data

Jordan, Apple.

Bird's best friend / by Apple Jordan. — 1st ed.
p. cm. — (Step into reading. Step 2 book)
At head of title: Up.

ISBN 978-0-7364-2579-7 (trade)
ISBN 978-0-7364-8066-6 (lib. bdg.)

I. Up (Motion picture) II. Title. PZ7.J755Bir 2009
[E]—dc22 2008039421

Printed in the United States of America   10 9 8 7 6 5 4 3   First Edition

Bird's Best Friend

By Apple Jordan

Illustrated by Caroline Egan, Olga Mosqueda,
Elena Naggi, and Scott Tilley

Random House 🏠 New York

Russell was

a Wilderness Explorer.

He was a friend to all.

He liked to help animals.

He liked to help people, too.

Russell wanted to help
a man named Carl.
Carl did not need help.

Carl was going on a trip.
He was moving his house
to the jungle.
He used balloons
to make the house float.

Russell was on
the porch.
He floated away, too.

The house flew
through a storm.
Russell helped
steer the house.

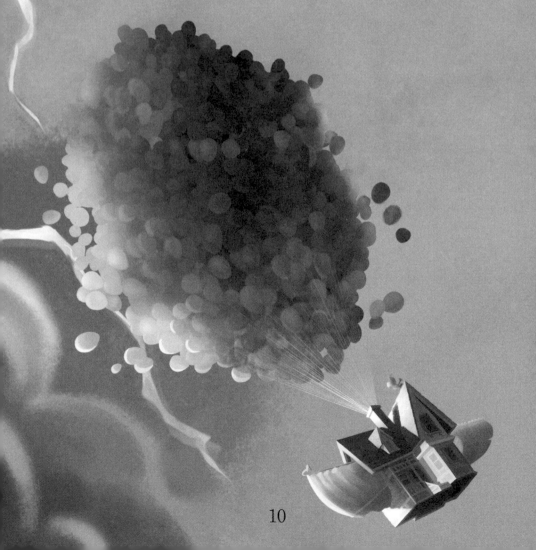

The house landed
in the jungle.
Russell helped
pull the house.

In the jungle,
Russell met a bird.
The bird
liked chocolate.

The bird liked Russell,
too.

She followed
Russell everywhere.
Russell and the bird
became best friends.

Soon they met

a dog named Dug.

Dug was there
to catch the bird!
Dug followed her.

Russell wanted
to protect the bird.
He asked Carl for help.

The bird's family
was far away.
Russell wanted
to get her home.

But a man named Muntz
wanted the bird.

Muntz's mean dogs
chased the bird.
Russell and Carl
helped her escape.

Muntz trapped
Russell, Carl, and the bird.

Muntz took the bird.

Russell was very sad.

Russell wanted
to help the bird.
He went after her.

Carl and Dug wanted

to help, too.

Russell, Carl, and Dug
saved the bird.

They took her home.

Russell really was

a bird's best friend!